ie	J
j	Or
ee	Ie
oa	Ai
or	Ee
ai	Oa

Jaiden painted an oak tree and got green paint on his top.

“Paint stains, Jaiden!” cried Dad.

Abigail
did it.

But Abigail did not paint.

Jaiden had a toffee...
...or ten.

“Jaiden!” moaned Dad.

Jet did it!

But Jet is just a dog.
(a black labrador)

Jaiden spilled popcorn on Dad's rug.

Jaiden,
pick it up!

Jaiden did it!
But Abigail...